The Secret

Sarah made her way to math class and sank into her seat. She tried to listen to Ms. Wyler but the problems on the blackboard seemed to run together and her eyes just wouldn't stay open. The teacher's voice seemed far away.

"Sarah!"

Sarah jerked, lifting her head off the desk. "I'm here, I mean—what did you say?"

The young teacher was frowning. "This is not the time for a nap! I think you'd better pay attention. Your work this week has hardly been satisfactory."

"Yes, Ms. Wyler," Sarah said. Several of the other students stared at her curiously. Sarah wished she could sink through the floor.

The teacher walked back to the front of the class and continued with the lesson. Sarah tried her best to stay awake but she felt her head drooping again.

"Sarah?" The whisper came from beside her. She looked across the aisle at Elizabeth Wakefield. "Is anything wrong?" Elizabeth asked.

Sarah shook her head. "No," she whispered back. "Nothing special."

If only she could tell Elizabeth the truth. But that was impossible!

Bantam Skylark Books in the SWEET VALLEY TWINS series
Ask your bookseller for the books you have missed.

#1 BEST FRIENDS
#2 TEACHER'S PET
#3 THE HAUNTED HOUSE
#4 CHOOSING SIDES
#5 SNEAKING OUT
#6 THE NEW GIRL
#7 THREE'S A CROWD
#8 FIRST PLACE
#9 AGAINST THE RULES
#10 ONE OF THE GANG
#11 BURIED TREASURE
#12 KEEPING SECRETS
#13 STRETCHING THE TRUTH
#14 TUG OF WAR
#15 THE OLDER BOY
#16 SECOND BEST
#17 BOYS AGAINST GIRLS
#18 CENTER OF ATTENTION
#19 THE BULLY
#20 PLAYING HOOKY
#21 LEFT BEHIND

Sweet Valley Twins Super Editions

#1 THE CLASS TRIP

SWEET VALLEY TWINS

Left Behind

Written by
Jamie Suzanne

Created by
FRANCINE PASCAL

A BANTAM SKYLARK BOOK®
TORONTO · NEW YORK · LONDON · SYDNEY · AUCKLAND

RL 4, 008–012

LEFT BEHIND
A Bantam Skylark Book / August 1988

*Produced by Daniel Weiss Associates, Inc.
27 West 20th Street
New York, NY 10011*

Cover art by James Mathewuse.

ISBN 0-553-15609-8

Published simultaneously in the United States and Canada

PRINTED IN THE UNITED STATES OF AMERICA

O   0 9 8 7 6 5 4 3

To Jaclyn Moritz

One

◇

Elizabeth Wakefield pushed through the big double doors of Sweet Valley Middle School and paused on the steps outside. She took a deep breath and let the warm California breeze blow through her long blond hair. It was a beautiful Friday afternoon and she felt wonderful.

"Hey, Elizabeth. Wait for us!"

Elizabeth turned and saw her best friend, Amy Sutton, coming out of school. She was followed by Sarah Thomas, a small girl with short brown hair who had the same math and history classes as she did. Amy was waving the latest edition of *The Sweet Valley Sixers*.

"Everyone loves this issue of the paper," Amy said. "We really did a good job with it."

"Now that this edition is out, it's time to start catching up on our schoolwork," Elizabeth said. "Are you guys ready to tackle our history project?"

Amy nodded. "Sarah and I were just talking about it. We have to pick a subject."

"We'd better make up our minds soon. It's due in less than two weeks," Elizabeth said.

"Let's not start until Monday," Amy suggested. "Who wants to work on the weekend?"

"OK," Elizabeth agreed. "I've got lots of plans for this Saturday and Sunday anyway."

"Not me. I hate weekends," Sarah said sadly.

The other two girls looked at her in surprise. Sarah flushed and looked away.

"Why?" Amy asked.

Sarah didn't answer. Elizabeth recalled hearing Sarah complain about weekends several times before, and she wondered how anyone could hate them. But looking at her friend's unhappy face, she knew it was time to change the subject.

"We've got plenty of time to work next week," she said. "So we'll start Monday. But let's pick a topic now."

"Good idea," Amy said. "What about the Civil War?"

Elizabeth shook her head. "At least three groups are already working on that. And lots of the boys are doing World War II, so let's skip that one, too."

"Colonial America?" Amy said.

"Maybe," Elizabeth answered.

"I have an idea," Sarah said. "What about the gold rush? That's almost local—I mean, it happened in California. I bet we could find lots of material about it."

"That's a great idea, Sarah," Elizabeth said. "Let's check out some books for research and plan to meet Monday after school."

The other two girls nodded.

"Hey," Sarah said, suddenly sounding excited. "Would you two like to spend next Friday night at my house? We could finish putting our project together then."

"That's fine with me," Amy said.

"What a great idea, Sarah. Then we could mix work with fun," Elizabeth said. "It's a deal."

"Do you guys want to come over to my house now?" Amy asked. "Mom promised to bake some brownies today."

"Sure, I'll come," Elizabeth nodded. "Mrs. Sutton makes the greatest brownies, Sarah. Can you come?"

"I can't," Sarah said. "I'm late already." She adjusted her knapsack and turned to go. "I'll see you Monday," she called, hurrying off.

"That's strange," Amy said. "Why do you think Sarah ran off so quickly?"

"I don't know," Elizabeth said. "Maybe she had other plans." Shaking her head, she followed Amy across the lawn.

"Lizzie, Amy, wait up." Jessica Wakefield ran swiftly down the steps.

"Hi, Jess," Elizabeth greeted her twin. "I thought you'd be gone by now. You're usually the first one out the door on Friday afternoons."

Unlike her sister, who loved school, Jessica couldn't wait to socialize with her friends. Although the girls were identical twins, sometimes it was hard to believe they were even related. They both had long blond hair, blue-green eyes, and a dimple in their left cheeks. But underneath, the twins were very different.

Elizabeth liked to read and hoped to be a writer some day. Writing for the sixth-grade newspaper was just a beginning. Jessica, on the other hand, thought newspaper work was dull. She preferred to spend time with her friends in the Unicorn Club, an exclusive group made up of the most popular girls. Elizabeth was convinced they spent all their time gossiping about boys and clothes. And she had absolutely no interest in becoming a member. But in spite of their very different personalities, the twins were still best friends.

"I stayed late to get the newest issue of *The Sweet Valley Sixers*," Jessica said. "I wanted to see the article about the Unicorn Club. It's not bad, but you could have said more about how special the club is."

"And how pretty and popular all the members are," Elizabeth teased.

"Yes." Jessica sounded perfectly serious.

Elizabeth couldn't hold back her laughter. "I'm the editor, Jess. I have to make sure our paper covers *all* the news," she reminded her twin.

"Well, the article could have been a little longer," Jessica said. "Anyway guess what, Lizzie? Janet Howell wants to get together with *me* after school to talk about ideas for a big Unicorn party. Isn't that great? She must have been impressed with me when I told her that the article in the paper was all my idea."

Elizabeth laughed and shook her head. Jessica

was constantly trying to impress Janet Howell. Janet was the president of the Unicorn Club and one of the most popular eighth graders. "That's nice, Jess. Are you going over to Janet's house?"

Jessica shook her head. "No. Janet said she'd come to our house. Oh, no! That reminds me."

"What's wrong?"

"I've got to run home and straighten up my bedroom," Jessica wailed. "It's a mess."

Elizabeth laughed, knowing that Jessica's bed was probably hidden somewhere underneath a pile of clothes, magazines, and candy wrappers. "Anyone who can make you clean your room can't be all bad," she murmured.

"Coming?" Jessica called over her shoulder as she started across the lawn.

"I'm going over to Amy's," Elizabeth answered, "to discuss our history project. I'll see you later."

As she and Amy headed across the lawn, Elizabeth thought of Sarah and wondered why weekends made her so miserable.

Two

◇

Jessica broke into a run as she raced up the driveway to her house. She reached inside the zipper pocket of her purple knapsack for her key, but found only a jumbled wad of notes that she had exchanged with Lila Fowler during English class that morning. When she finally located her house key, she let herself in and hurried upstairs to her room.

As usual, her pink-and-white bedroom was a mess. The bed was unmade and covered with clothes. Jessica sighed. She was in no mood to straighten up, but if she wanted to impress Janet, she didn't have much choice. She quickly straightened up, then ran into the bathroom that connected her room with Elizabeth's.

She pulled a comb through her thick blond hair and headed for the kitchen to see what she could offer her guest. Just as she reached the bottom of the stairs, the doorbell rang.

Jessica ran to open the door. "Janet! I didn't think you'd be here so soon."

"Well, I couldn't wait to hear your ideas," Janet said. "Even if you are only a sixth grader."

Jessica was so excited to have Janet to herself that she didn't even notice the put-down.

"You've been such a valuable addition to the Unicorn Club," Janet continued, more graciously. "I just know you'll have some super ideas."

"I'm so glad you think so," Jessica said. "Would you like a snack?"

Looking around the kitchen, Jessica was relieved to see that her mother had left them a big plate of oatmeal cookies. Thank goodness she'd gotten home before Steven, her fourteen-year-old brother. He had a reputation as a bottomless pit when it came to eating. He liked eating almost as much as he liked playing basketball.

"Is Steven home?" Janet asked, almost as if she

had been thinking the same thing. "I thought he might be here."

Jessica shook her head. "No," she said. "Good thing, too. Otherwise the cookies would have been all gone." She poured a glass of milk for each of them, then sat down at the table beside Janet.

"What kind of party should we have?" Janet took a bite of a cookie. "We've had plenty of pool and costume parties. I want to do something really different this time."

"I know!" Jessica said. "What about a luau? I saw a great show on TV last night all about a traditional Hawaiian feast." She paused and looked at Janet to see if the older girl approved.

"Sounds interesting." Janet grabbed a second cookie from the plate. "Tell me more."

"We could wear leis—you know, those flower necklaces—and play Hawaiian music. My dad has an old ukulele he might let us borrow."

"But Jessica, where would we get the leis? Even if we could make them, it would take us hours and hours, and flowers are really expensive. Besides, who wants to sit around making boring necklaces?"

Jessica shrugged. Planning was her specialty,

not carrying out the details. "Well, we could form a decorations committee," she suggested. "Get some other Unicorns to work on that. Ellen, Tamara, and maybe Grace."

Janet nodded. "Good thinking," she said. "And you know, when I walked up to your house, I noticed some big palm trees in your backyard. Do you think your parents would let us have the party here?"

Jessica beamed, thrilled with the unexpected honor. "At our house? Oh, I'm sure my parents would agree," she said, thinking, *They have to say yes! They just have to.*

"Let's go out back and see how much room you have," Janet suggested. "Then we can decide how many people to invite."

Jessica nodded. They left the kitchen, walked through the living room and went outside through the sliding glass doors.

Janet looked over the patio and the pool. *She was right*, Jessica thought. *The tall palm trees in the backyard would make a perfect backdrop for an outdoor Hawaiian feast.*

"What should we have to eat?" Janet wondered aloud.

Jessica couldn't believe that Janet, an eighth

grader, was accepting all of her suggestions. *Of course, I'm always good with parties,* she reminded herself.

"At real luaus, they have roasted pigs on stakes," she remembered. "But I don't think my dad would let us dig a hole in the yard."

They looked at the smooth, even lawn.

To her relief, Janet shook her head. "I don't like pork, and that would be too much trouble, anyhow. I'd just as soon have pizza."

"We could always stick some pineapple on top," Jessica said.

They both laughed.

Janet is finally beginning to appreciate me, Jessica thought. *I bet she'll recommend me for Unicorn Club president when she graduates from the middle school!*

The two girls sat beside the pool and talked about the luau until it was almost dark.

Janet looked at her watch. "I guess I'd better be going," she said. She sounded strangely reluctant. *Wow,* Jessica thought. *She's having such a good time she doesn't want to leave.*

They stood up and walked through the house. The sound of running water could be heard in the kitchen.

"Is someone here?" Janet asked. "Maybe it's Steven."

Jessica paused to look into the kitchen. "No, it's my mother," she said. "Hi, Mom."

Mrs. Wakefield was standing at the sink washing lettuce. "Hello, dear. How was school?"

"Fine. This is Janet Howell," Jessica said. "One of my friends from school."

Mrs. Wakefield smiled at them both. "I'm always glad to meet Jessica's friends. Would you like to stay for dinner, Janet? We're having pork chops and scalloped potatoes."

Janet's eyes brightened, but Jessica hurried to spare her any embarrassment. "She can't tonight, Mom."

"Maybe another time, then," Mrs. Wakefield said.

Jessica pulled Janet toward the front porch, whispering, "I remembered that you don't like pork!"

Janet frowned. "Oh, right. Thanks," she said. "Where's the rest of your family?"

"Elizabeth is over at Amy's," Jessica said.

"And Steven?"

Jessica shrugged. "Oh, he's probably still at basketball practice. Hey, Janet, is anything wrong?" Jessica asked when she noticed how unhappy Janet looked.

"No, no." Janet shook her head. "I think we should meet one more time, Jessica. There are still a lot of party details to discuss."

"Sure." Jessica was only too happy to agree. "Want me to come to your house after school on Monday?"

"No," Janet answered quickly. "I mean, we're having our kitchen painted, and my mother doesn't want anyone in the house. You understand."

"Sure," Jessica said. "We can always meet here. We can talk in my room if we need privacy."

"I don't mind having your family around. Maybe Steven will have some good ideas," Janet said, halfway out the front door. "Talk to you soon."

"You bet." Jessica waved as Janet headed down the driveway.

She was so pleased about her new friendship with Janet that she didn't even complain when her mother asked her to set the table.

When Elizabeth got home, she was surprised to see the dinner table already set. And Jessica, instead of complaining that she had had to do all the chores, greeted her sister with a big smile.

"Better hurry. Dinner's almost ready."

"What's up?" Elizabeth stared at her twin.

"Why are you in such a good mood?"

"You'll see." Jessica's smile was smug.

"You'll never guess what happened today," she said when the entire Wakefield family was seated at the dining room table for dinner.

"You got an A on your history test," Mr. Wakefield guessed.

Steven chuckled. "Fat chance. My guess is some boy winked at her in the cafeteria."

"You're both wrong." Jessica made a face at her brother. "Janet Howell asked *me* to help plan the next Unicorn party."

She paused, waiting for a reaction, but nobody said a word. Mr. Wakefield merely raised his brows and took another bite of salad. Mrs. Wakefield smiled, and Steven laughed out loud. "Is that all?" he said. "I thought it was something important."

"It *is* important!" Jessica's voice rose. "You don't know anything," she grumbled to her brother.

Elizabeth tried to explain. "Janet Howell's a very popular eighth grader, and she's also president of the Unicorn Club."

"She's very important," Jessica added. "Besides, she's nice and I like her."

"Well, I think that's wonderful, dear," Mrs. Wakefield said, smiling.

"And she liked my idea about having a Hawaiian luau," Jessica went on. "Is it all right if we have the party in our backyard? It's the perfect spot. We've got palm trees, and the pool, and everything." She looked anxiously at her parents, who exchanged glances. To her relief, her mother answered promptly.

"Of course, honey. You know your friends are always welcome at our house."

"As long as you and Elizabeth do your share of the preparations," Mr. Wakefield added. "It shouldn't fall on your mother's shoulders, you know."

"I will," Jessica agreed. "But who said anything about Elizabeth?"

"Thanks a lot, Jess." Elizabeth frowned at her sister.

Steven hooted. "You've done it now," he muttered under his breath.

Jessica stuck out her tongue at him.

But looking at her parents, she saw that both were regarding her sternly.

"You could hardly have a party at home and not invite your own sister," Mr. Wakefield said.

"Elizabeth doesn't care about the Unicorns," Jessica explained. "She doesn't even like them."

"Then maybe Elizabeth would like to invite

some of her own friends," Mrs. Wakefield suggested. "That would solve the problem."

"But then it won't be a Unicorn party!" Jessica wailed.

Mr. and Mrs. Wakefield ignored her protest. "I'm sure you two can find a happy compromise," Mrs. Wakefield said. "Now, who's ready for chocolate pudding?"

"I am!" Steven cried out.

Jessica stared down at her plate, her thoughts gloomy. How could she convince her parents that Elizabeth shouldn't come to her party? Glancing over at her sister, she added to herself, *And how can I convince Elizabeth?*

Three

◇

On Saturday morning Jessica slept late. When she finally came downstairs, Elizabeth and Steven were at the kitchen table, finishing off a stack of pancakes.

"Hey, save some for me," Jessica called, hurrying to sit down.

Mrs. Wakefield set a full plate in front of her. "Good morning, sleepyhead."

"Hi, Mom. Thanks." Jessica said, taking a big bite.

"I thought you were going to sleep all day," Elizabeth said. "We're leaving for the skating rink soon."

"Oh, I almost forgot." Jessica's blue-green eyes lit up with sudden inspiration. "Mom said we could each invite one friend to the skating rink, right? Maybe I should ask Janet."

Elizabeth looked at her sister in surprise. "I thought you were going to invite Lila."

"I was," Jessica admitted. "But when I mentioned it at lunch yesterday, she said she might go shopping today." Jessica threw down her napkin. "I'm going to call Janet and see if she'd like to go."

"We'll pick her up at twelve-thirty," Mrs. Wakefield called over her daughter's back. "Who did you invite, Elizabeth?"

"Amy," Elizabeth said. "She's a great skater."

Steven stood up from the table. "Great breakfast, Mom," he said. "I'm going to the park to shoot some hoops with the guys."

Elizabeth put her plate in the dishwasher and then ran upstairs to her bedroom. Since there was so much time before she went skating, she decided to start her new Amanda Howard mystery. She was halfway through the first chapter when Jessica came bursting through her bedroom door.

"Janet's coming with us, Lizzie," she bubbled happily. "I think she really likes me."

"Why shouldn't she?" Elizabeth said. "Lots of girls like you."

"But Janet's so popular and important. And she's in the eighth grade."

"Well then, maybe she just likes to skate," Elizabeth said with a giggle.

"Very funny, Elizabeth. Janet's more fun than Amy Sutton any day! Oh, by the way, Amy's on the phone for you."

"Why didn't you say so?" Elizabeth jumped up, dropping her book. "I didn't hear the phone ring."

She hurried out to the phone in the hallway. "Amy? What's up?"

"Elizabeth, I hate to tell you this—"

"What?"

"I can't go skating this afternoon." Amy sounded so gloomy that Elizabeth tried to stifle her own sigh of disappointment. "You're not sick, are you?" she asked.

"No, but Mrs. Nelson next door has to go to the doctor, and she asked if I would watch her little boy."

"I understand," Elizabeth assured her friend. "Do you know if Julie is around? Maybe I'll invite her."

"She went out of town with her family this weekend," Amy reminded her.

"Oh, that's right." Elizabeth thought about who else she might call. "Does Sarah like to skate?"

"I don't know," Amy said, "but you could ask. I've got her phone number."

Elizabeth scribbled the number on a pad near the phone. "Thanks, Amy. I'll give Sarah a call right now. Bye."

She dialed the number and waited for someone to answer.

"Hello?"

"Sarah? This is Elizabeth Wakefield. Would you like to go roller-skating with me this afternoon?"

After a short pause, Sarah answered. "I'd love to go, but I don't know if I can. My dad and—my dad's gone shopping, and I don't have a way to get there."

"That's no problem. My mom will pick you up," Elizabeth offered. "And it's our treat."

"Thanks, Elizabeth." Sarah sounded more excited now. "Sure, I'll go."

"Great. We'll see you in half an hour," Elizabeth promised. "It'll be fun."

Jessica bent over her skate, trying to untangle the knot in her laces. "Darn it," she muttered to herself, glancing toward the big indoor rink. Janet stood by the smooth wooden floor, already laced into her rented skates and ready to go.

Jessica pulled at the wearisome knot, but her frenzied tugging only seemed to make it more secure.

"Need help, Jess?" Elizabeth asked, coming up behind her twin.

"Thanks, Lizzie." Jessica breathed a sigh of relief and let Elizabeth coax the knot out of the lace. When Elizabeth was done, Jessica laced up her skates and stood up. She wavered for a brief moment and then quickly found her balance. She entered the rink and skated smoothly toward the center with Janet behind her.

Elizabeth watched her go, then turned to Sarah, who was adjusting a rented pair of skates. "Do those fit all right?"

Sarah nodded. "I used to have my own skates," she told Elizabeth. "But they're too little now. My father was going to buy me a new pair, but when my mother died he became really forgetful."

Elizabeth looked at Sarah in surprise. "I didn't know your mother had died," she said. "I'm sorry."

No wonder Sarah looks sad sometimes, Elizabeth thought.

Sarah bent over her skates to hide her face. Her voice quavered as she began to speak. "Right after she died, my dad used to spend a lot of time with me. We did lots of things together. We had picnics in the park, we went to the movies, we shopped for groceries. Now everything's different."

Elizabeth looked at Sarah closely. "Why? What happened?"

Sarah sniffed and wiped her eyes. "Annie, my dad's girlfriend, came into the picture. They're getting married in a few months. She acts nice to me when Dad's around. But the minute he's gone, she changes. I don't think she really likes me."

Sarah stood up, and Elizabeth followed her onto the rink. "Are you sure?" she asked. "Maybe she does like you, and she just doesn't know how to show it."

"I don't know, Elizabeth. I used to think she liked me a lot," Sarah confided. "She's pretty young and she likes the same music I do and wears really nice clothes. I thought she was great, at first. She showed me how to wear my hair and taught me how to put on eye makeup. She even went shopping with me and my dad and helped me pick out a bunch of outfits."

"So what went wrong?" Elizabeth asked.

"We don't ever have fun anymore," Sarah said. "I can't do anything right. When we go to the movies, she yells at me for spilling popcorn. At the park,

I run too quickly or I walk too slowly. I hate to go anywhere with her and my father, because I just know I'll manage to do something wrong."

"What about your father? Have you told him how you feel?" Elizabeth asked.

Sarah shook her head. "He barely notices me anymore, and it hurts my feelings. I don't know how to make him understand how I feel. He'll just think I'm being jealous. I'm dreading their wedding, Elizabeth. After that, Annie will be with us forever!"

Across the rink, Jessica and Janet skated around in leisurely circles. "I'm not going too slowly for you, am I, Jessica?" Janet asked.

"Oh, no, not at all," Jessica answered sweetly. The truth was that Jessica would have preferred to go much faster. Steven had once called her the terror of the rink.

"Steven's been teaching me a lot of fancy stuff," she told Janet. "You should see him though; he's much better than I am on skates."

Janet's eyes lit up. "Do you think he might come to the rink today?"

Jessica rolled her eyes. "He went to the park. He's a basketball fanatic."

Janet looked disappointed. "You could have told me, Jessica. I thought your whole family was coming."

"What difference does it make?" Jessica stared at Janet in disbelief.

Janet shrugged. "Never mind. Let's get something to drink."

"You don't want to skate?" Jessica asked. She was hoping that someone from school would see her skating with Janet Howell. After all, it wasn't every day that she hung out with an eighth grader!

"Oh, the rink's awfully crowded."

Jessica looked around the half-empty rink, but she didn't want to contradict Janet. "Okay," she agreed. "I'm thirsty, too."

They skated toward the snack bar at the other end of the building. While they stood in line, Jessica heard familiar voices behind her. She looked over her shoulder and was delighted to see Bruce Patman and Rick Hunter, both seventh graders at Sweet Valley Middle School. They were with Danny Jacobson, an eighth grader, and another boy Jessica didn't know. They all were clustered around the video arcade games.

"Hi, Janet," Danny called. "What are you doing here?"

"Skating, what do you think? How come you don't have skates on? Are you too busy saving the galaxy?"

"You bet!" Danny answered. "I'm up to fifty thousand points on *Star Smasher.*"

"Wow!" Jessica batted her long lashes at the older boy. "That's great."

"Thanks, um—" The good-looking eighth grader hesitated.

"Jessica," she told him. "Jessica Wakefield."

"Oh, yeah." He nodded. "See you girls around."

He turned back to the video game, and Jessica was sure she had made a favorable impression. Danny was awfully cute! And he must have thought she was very mature after seeing her hanging around with Janet.

When the two girls finally reached the front of the line, the counter clerk asked, "What do you want?"

"Cherry cola," Janet said.

Jessica was about to ask for lemonade, but she quickly changed her order. "Cherry cola for me, too," she said. "Want to share some popcorn, Janet?"

The eighth grader shook her head. "I don't like popcorn. Maybe some nachos."

Jessica sniffed the buttery smell of the freshly popped corn, then reluctantly agreed. "OK."

They carried their food to a small table and sat down. Jessica took a deep breath. Making Janet think she was mature and sophisticated was hard work!

But when Janet turned and whispered, "Did you hear who Tamara Chase went to the movies with last night?" Jessica knew it was all worth it.

Four

◇

When Mrs. Wakefield dropped Sarah off in front of her house, the girl turned to wave to Elizabeth and Jessica. She was in no hurry to go inside. Annie would probably still be there.

She entered the front hall and listened for the sound of her dad's voice. Instead she heard Annie chattering to someone on the telephone. She tried to sneak silently up the old staircase. But the bottom step creaked the moment she placed her weight on it.

"Who's there?" Annie called out.

Sarah sighed. Reluctantly she turned back toward the living room. Annie was curled up on the end of the sofa, the phone perched on her shoulder as she painted her long nails a vibrant red. Several magazines were scattered around the floor, and a bag of chocolate cookies lay open on the coffee table in front of her.

"What are you sneaking in like that for?" Annie demanded, her pretty face drawn up into a scowl.

"I wasn't," Sarah answered. "Where's Dad? I thought you and Dad were going shopping."

Annie looked even more irritated. "We were supposed to, but at the last minute his office called and he ended up going in to work. All that man ever does is work!"

Sarah couldn't wait to escape to her room. Annie was definitely not in a good mood. "Well, I'm going upstairs," she said.

"Wait. Not yet," Annie commanded. "I was going to put away the lunch dishes, but my nails aren't dry yet. Why don't you be a doll and do it for me? Unless you're too good to do a few extra chores, that is."

"Of course not," Sarah murmured. She hurried toward the kitchen.

"Good," Annie said complacently. "After all the years I've worked, I deserve some relaxation!"

Out of the corner of her eye, Sarah saw Annie

wave her wet nails in the air. The large diamond-and-ruby-ring on her left hand flashed, and her matching diamond-and-ruby earrings sparkled in the afternoon sunlight. The sweater she wore was new and came from the most expensive boutique in the Valley Mall.

You don't like Daddy working, Sarah thought, *but you don't seem to mind spending his money!* She didn't have the nerve to speak her thought aloud, though.

As she entered the kitchen, she noticed that Annie hadn't even cleared off the table after breakfast. Dirty plates and glasses sat on the place mats, and crumbs littered the tile floor.

Sarah scraped and rinsed the plates, then loaded them carefully into the dishwasher. She took a sponge and wiped off the sticky table, then swept the floor. She had just finished when she heard the sound of a car in the driveway.

"Are you through in there?" Annie called.

Sarah put away the broom and came into the hall. She was just in time to see Annie toss her bottle of nail polish into her purse, fluff the couch pillows, and straighten up the mess on the floor.

Sarah blinked. Her father would never know how sneaky Annie could be.

When the front door opened, Sarah ran to hug

her father. Mr. Thomas quickly kissed the top of her head.

Annie, standing behind Sarah, got a long kiss. "Have you girls been keeping busy?" Mr. Thomas asked.

"Of course," Annie said.

Sarah made a face. She had been busy, but Annie certainly hadn't been. Her father didn't seem to notice her expression.

"Did you take care of all your boring business?" Annie was asking him.

"For the moment. But something urgent has come up in Texas. "I'm going to have to leave Monday morning to straighten out some accounts."

"Oh, no! That's awful," Annie pouted.

Sarah felt her heart beat faster. "How long will you be gone?" she asked. Her voice came out high and shrill.

Her father set his briefcase down by the hall table and put one arm around her. "I'm afraid I'll have to be away for a whole week. I'll be back early Sunday."

"That long?" Sarah wanted to cry. It was bad enough that she never got to be alone with her dad anymore. Now he'd be gone for seven long days. "Is Aunt Lillian going to stay with me?"

Mr. Thomas smiled at her. "No need for her to come all the way from Denver. I thought this would be a good chance for you and Annie to get to know each other better. After all, Annie will be moving in for good very soon. What do you think, sweetheart? You can stay here, can't you?" He put his arm around Annie.

She looked up at him lovingly, but said, "I did have some things planned for this week."

Mr. Thomas looked surprised. "Oh, well. I just thought you'd enjoy staying here with Sarah," he said. "You've often said how much you're looking forward to spending more time with her."

"And I am." Annie smiled at them both. "I'll just change my plans." She patted Sarah on the head, but her blue eyes looked right through her. Sarah was certain that Annie wasn't any more pleased about Dad's idea than she was.

"Then it's all settled," Mr. Thomas said. "I'm sure you and Annie will find plenty of things to do together."

Sarah bit her lip and tried to hold back her tears. What was she going to do?

"Are we going out for dinner, Robbie?" Annie asked. "Let's go to that little sushi place that I like so much."

Sarah felt her stomach turn over just thinking about sushi. She stared up at her father with a pleading look in her eyes.

Mr. Thomas shook his head at her. "Now, Sarah, you were out having fun with your friends this afternoon while Annie straightened up around here. It's only fair that she pick the restaurant."

He glanced down the hall toward the neat kitchen, and Annie smiled at his praise. Sarah didn't dare argue. Annie was always too quick for her.

"Then we can go see *The Midnight Murders*," Annie said. "I've heard it's so exciting."

Mr. Thomas looked concerned. "That movie is R-rated," he said. "I don't think Sarah would enjoy it."

"So? We can drop her back at the house," Annie pointed out. "She's not a baby, Rob."

Sarah felt her stomach turn over again. She hated staying by herself at night, and her father knew it.

Fortunately this time Mr. Thomas sounded firm. "I think we can find a movie that we'd all like to see," he answered.

Pouting, Annie flounced off to get her jacket.

Sarah felt heartened by this small victory. She took her father's hand. "Daddy, do you have to go away for such a long time?" she asked.

"It'll go by quickly," he promised. "You'll see."

Not quickly enough, Sarah thought as she tried to return his smile. She felt hollow inside. A whole week alone with Annie! She couldn't think of anything more horrible.

After dropping Sarah off, Mrs. Wakefield and the twins stopped at the deli to pick up some hero sandwiches for dinner.

When they arrived home, the girls jumped out of the car and carried the bags of food into the house. Jessica called the rest of the family to the table, and Elizabeth set out napkins and plates.

"Want to split this tuna sub?" Jessica asked her twin.

"All right," Elizabeth agreed. She accepted half of the big sandwich and helped herself to a pickle.

"Did you two have a good time at the skating rink?" Mr. Wakefield asked.

Elizabeth nodded. She had enjoyed skating. She just wished Sarah hadn't been so sad.

"It was great!" Jessica said. "You should have seen me skating with Janet. Everyone who saw me thought I was so mature."

Steven snickered.

Jessica threw him an indignant look. "They did.

There were some boys from school in the snack bar. They were very impressed to see me with Janet."

"Aha! The truth comes out," Steven said, grinning. "That's why you like hanging around Janet. More guys to pick from."

Jessica tossed her long hair back over her shoulder. "I can't help it if older boys find me interesting," she boasted. "It's because I'm so grown up for my age."

Steven laughed so hard that Jessica dropped her half-eaten sandwich onto her plate and glared at him.

"Grown up! You?" he hooted. "You must be joking. Janet's pulling your leg."

"She is not!" Jessica shrieked. "She likes me! Janet says—"

"*Janet says,*" Steven mocked. "Is that engraved on your brain?"

"Stop teasing your sister," Mr. Wakefield said sternly. "There's no reason Jessica can't be friendly with upperclassmen."

"Just remember that Janet *is* older than you, Jessica," Mrs. Wakefield said. "You can't expect to do everything an eighth grader does."

"Why not?" Jessica demanded. "Don't Janet and I have a lot in common, Lizzie?" she said.

Elizabeth, who had been thinking about Sarah, looked up. She wrinkled her nose. "I guess so," she said. "You're both Unicorns—"

"Snobs, you mean," Steven corrected.

"You both love clothes—"

"Clotheshorses," Steven said, snickering.

"You both like parties—" Elizabeth went on.

"Boy crazy," Steven translated.

"Mom!" Jessica threw her hands in the air. "Can't you stop him?"

Mrs. Wakefield pushed a plate toward her son. "Steven, have some more potato salad." Steven, diverted at last, spooned some onto his plate.

Jessica exhaled noisily and picked up her sandwich again. "Some people just don't understand me," she announced, glancing angrily at her brother. "But Janet says I'm very mature for my age."

Steven's mouth was too full for him to make a comment, but he winked across the table at the twins.

Jessica pretended not to notice.

Elizabeth smothered a giggle.

"Don't you think I'm mature, Mom?" Jessica said.

Mrs. Wakefield nodded, smiling a little.

"Told you." Jessica said with a smug look.

"Grab the cream puffs before Steven gets them, Jess," Elizabeth said. "Or we won't get any."

Elizabeth snatched the white bag away from Steven's outstretched fingers. Giggling, the two girls took their share of dessert.

Their parents smiled at each other across the table. "Don't worry, Steven," Mrs. Wakefield said. "We'll save one for you."

"Steven," Jessica snapped back, "Don't you think you're a little too grown up to be eating cream puffs?"

At that, all the Wakefields, except for Steven, started to laugh.

Five

◇

On Monday morning, Sarah followed her father out to his car. She watched him load his suitcases into the trunk, then gave him a big hug. "I'll miss you," she said, swallowing hard to force back a sob.

Mr. Thomas winked at her. "Come on, now. Give me a smile," he urged. "I'm sure you and Annie will get on just fine without me."

Sarah managed a feeble grin, but as soon as his car pulled out of the drive, her smile faded. The lump in her throat ached.

She walked back inside the house and gathered her schoolbooks. The phone rang just as she was about to leave, and she ran to the kitchen to answer it.

"Hello," Sarah said.

"Is Annie there?" a man asked.

Annie picked up the other extension. "I have the phone, Sarah," Annie said. "Hang up right now."

Sarah hung up the phone and went back to the hall table to get her books. As she opened the front door, Annie came down the staircase and said, "Sarah, wait just one minute. From now on, when the phone rings, *I'll* answer it. Understand?" Sarah nodded. "That was one of my old neighbors in Orange County. My little sister's very sick and my aunt can't take care of her alone. I'm going to have to go myself."

"I'm sorry about your sister," Sarah said. "I hope she feels better. Will you be home in time for dinner?"

"I've got to take care of her." Annie sounded exasperated. "I'll have to stay overnight."

"But I'll be all alone!" Sarah stared at Annie in dismay, feeling the knots in her stomach harden. "Can't I go with you?"

"And get sick yourself? Don't be silly," Annie scolded. "Nothing's going to happen to you while I'm gone. So stop worrying."

"OK," Sarah murmured, but the knots inside

her stomach twisted painfully. She had never spent a whole night in the house alone. "When will you be back?"

"I'll be back tomorrow night," Annie said. "And Sarah—"

Sarah had opened the front door, but she paused at the urgency in Annie's voice.

"What?"

"If your father calls, don't tell him I'm gone. It will just ruin his business trip."

"I won't," Sarah promised. As she pulled the door shut behind her, she thought to herself, *Monday is not getting off to a very good start.*

Uh oh, Jessica thought when she got to school and found an angry Lila Fowler waiting for her in front of her locker.

"I'm surprised you're willing to show your face in school," Lila said. She put her hands on her hips.

Jessica looked puzzled. "What are you talking about?"

"You were supposed to call me about skating on Saturday afternoon, remember?"

"But you said you might go shopping," Jessica protested. "So I asked someone else."

"I know you did!" Lila shouted. "Bruce Patman

told me all about seeing you and Janet. Janet doesn't even like to skate."

"She does, too," Jessica shouted back. "Anyway, I don't see why you're angry."

"Because *I'm* supposed to be your best friend," Lila pointed out, her brown eyes flashing.

"But Lila, I did ask you first. Since you didn't want to go, I just asked someone else," Jessica explained.

"I didn't say I didn't want to go. I said I wasn't sure."

"That's not what I remember," Jessica told her. "You don't have to be so snippy. The whole world doesn't revolve around you, Lila Fowler."

"That's a nice thing to say! Some friend you are!" Lila tossed her light brown hair over her shoulders. "I know you, Jessica. You're trying to impress my cousin just because she's older and president of the Unicorns."

"I am not!" But Jessica felt herself blush guiltily.

Lila's eyes widened. "That's it, isn't it? You sneak!"

"Take that back!" Jessica yelled.

The two girls glared at each other.

"Wow, what a fight!" Caroline Pearce said. The

red-haired girl stood just behind them. "Are you two going to start pulling each other's hair?"

Her interest in their fight shattered the two girls' angry mood. They turned their backs, and Caroline walked away, looking disappointed.

"Great," Jessica muttered. "Now everyone in school will hear about our fight. Caroline's got the biggest mouth in Sweet Valley."

"It's your own fault for being so inconsiderate," Lila said accusingly and then stomped off down the hall.

Jessica slammed her locker shut. Talk about selfish! Why did Lila think Jessica couldn't have any other friends?

She hurried down the hall, hoping to catch Janet before classes started.

Six

◇

The school day ended much too soon for Sarah. She dreaded going home. She spent an extra hour after school working on the history project with Elizabeth and Amy. But she was too distracted to get much work done. She walked home slowly, wishing she could spend the night somewhere else. But no one was allowed to have friends sleep over on a school night. And Annie would be furious if she found out Sarah had told someone why she didn't want to stay at home.

As Sarah approached her house she thought longingly of the days when her mother was there to greet her with a hug as she walked through the door.

The thought brought tears to her eyes. She brushed them away quickly, then dug out her house key and trudged up the long driveway. The hallway looked dark and empty, and all she could think of was the long night she had ahead of her!

The sudden shrill ringing of the phone made her jump. She ran to answer it.

"Hi, honey," her father said. It felt so good to hear his voice. "Just wanted you to know that I'm in Dallas. I'll be on the road quite a bit this week, so it will be hard for me to check in with you. I'll try to call again in a few days. Everything all right at home?"

Sarah wanted to say, *No, I'm lonely and scared.* But she had promised Annie she wouldn't tell. "Everything's fine," she said. "I miss you."

"I miss you, too, honey," he said. "Can I speak to Annie?"

Oh, no! What could she say? Sarah thought quickly. "She's taking a shower."

"Oh," Mr. Thomas said. "Well, tell her I called. You two have fun, but don't stay up too late. Remember, you have school tomorrow."

"I know, Daddy," Sarah said. She hung up the receiver and looked around the empty house. To her surprise, the phone rang again almost at once. She picked it up quickly. Had her father heard the unhappiness in her voice? Maybe he had decided to come right home.

But it wasn't him.

"Sarah? It's Aunt Lillian. How are you, darling?"

"I'm fine," Sarah lied. Aunt Lillian was her mother's sister and Sarah's favorite aunt. After Sarah's mother had died, Aunt Lillian had suggested that Mr. Thomas send Sarah to Denver to live with her. But Mr. Thomas had refused, and even though Sarah loved her aunt, she was glad. She didn't want to lose her father, too!

Sarah tried to keep the anxiety out of her voice as she answered the usual questions about school.

"Are you and Annie getting along OK?" Aunt Lillian asked.

"Of course," Sarah said quickly. She had never complained to her aunt about her soon-to-be stepmother, but somehow Aunt Lillian seemed to sense her discomfort.

"Well, as long as you're happy," her aunt said. "I can't wait for your next visit, dear. I have so many things planned."

"I'm looking forward to it, too," Sarah said. "I've got to go and fix dinner now, Aunt Lillian."

"You're fixing dinner?"

"Oh, Annie and I are making dinner. I like to help," Sarah said quickly.

"Well, be careful, dear," her aunt warned. "Are you sure you're all right? You don't sound very happy. You know, dear, you're always welcome to stay here."

"Thanks, Aunt Lillian," Sarah murmured, near tears. She wished she could tell her aunt how she really felt. "But I'm fine."

"OK, dear. I'll talk to you soon. Goodbye."

Sarah was glad to hang up the phone. Lying to everyone was hard and left her feeling guilty and uneasy. Thank goodness Annie would be back tomorrow! Then she could stop pretending. Right now she had to decide what to have for dinner.

She went into the kitchen and reheated a bowl of spaghetti in the microwave, then made a small salad and sat down to eat. When she was done, she washed the dishes slowly while she thought about how to spend the rest of her long evening.

"First I'll do my homework," Sarah told herself virtuously. "Then I'll take a bath, watch one television show, and go to bed."

Her plan sounded sensible and mature, the sort of schedule a girl old enough to stay alone would make. Sarah just wished she felt as grown-up as she sounded!

She carried her schoolbooks into the kitchen and spread her math homework out on the table. But as soon as she sat down, she found she couldn't concentrate. When the sun went down, the house grew very dark, and Sarah began to hear sounds all around her.

"It's nothing," she muttered to herself, trying to concentrate on her long division. But the creaking noises seemed to get louder.

She jumped up from the kitchen table and walked around the first floor of the house, flipping on a light switch in every room. When the downstairs was flooded with light, she felt a little better. But even then it was hard to think about going upstairs. The second floor looked so vacant and dark.

Sarah collected her books, checked the locks on the front and back doors, and slowly worked her way up the stairs. She felt a little better when she reached her own room. She was able to finish her math homework and read a chapter in her history book.

When all her homework was done, she went into the bathroom and ran a warm bath. She lowered herself into the steamy water and tried to relax. But a creak from the downstairs hall made her drop her bar of soap. She told herself it was just the pipes, but it was no use. She trembled at every little sound. She hurried through her bath and pulled on her pajamas.

It was too difficult to go back downstairs to watch television, so Sarah got into bed, leaving all the lights on. She looked around the room, then got back out of bed to grab two of her favorite stuffed animals off the bookcase. Clutching an ancient teddy bear and a large gold lion, she finally snuggled down under the covers.

If only her dad were home. If only Annie were here. Anyone familiar would do. Sighing, Sarah pulled herself into a ball and closed her eyes, reminding herself that it would be morning soon.

The night seemed to last forever. She couldn't sleep with the light shining in her eyes. Even her small bedside lamp seemed too bright. But if she turned off the light. . . She shuddered at the thought. She finally crawled out of bed and dug through her dresser drawers until she found the night-light she'd used when she was small. She plugged the tiny appliance into a socket near her bed and switched the other lights off. Then she got back into bed, pulled the covers over her head again and squeezed her eyes shut.

When the first signs of daylight appeared through the drawn shades, she gave up trying to sleep. Yawning, she crawled wearily out of bed. She didn't feel rested at all. How could she possibly face school today?

Well, anything is better than staying alone in this big, empty house, she thought. She splashed cold water on her face, rubbed her bloodshot eyes, and went to her closet to find something to wear.

At school, Mr. Nydick's history class seemed to last forever. Sarah liked the teacher, but today she discovered that his low voice lulled her awfully close to sleep. She caught herself twice just as her head began to nod.

When lunchtime came, Sarah was too tired to be hungry. All she wanted was to go to sleep. But she trudged on toward the cafeteria.

She took her tray to the back of the room, looking for a quiet spot to sit. The loud hum of voices in the big room made her head ache.

"Sarah," someone called. "Over here."

Sarah turned slowly and saw Amy and Elizabeth waving at her. She carried her tray over and sat down beside them, managing a smile. Picking up her sandwich, she decided she was really too tired to eat.

"What's the matter?" Elizabeth asked. "Don't you feel well, Sarah?"

"I have a headache," Sarah said truthfully.

"Why don't you go to the school nurse?" Elizabeth urged.

Sarah thought of the cot up in the nurse's office. She could lie down there—what a wonderful thought! But her pleasure faded quickly. The nurse would call home to tell her father she was sick. Then her secret would be exposed. Worst of all, Annie would be very angry. The last thing she needed was to make Annie angry.

Sarah sighed. "I'm OK," she told her friends.

"You don't look OK," Elizabeth pointed out, exchanging a troubled glance with Amy.

Sarah was just too tired to argue.

Seven

"I don't know what's wrong with Sarah," Elizabeth said. She and Jessica were in the Wakefield's kitchen having an after-school snack. "I'm worried about her, Jess. She was acting so strangly today. When Amy and I tried to talk to her during lunch, she was really out of it."

"Uh-huh." Jessica nodded and reached for another chocolate-chip cookie. "I wish Janet had come home with me today. We still have so much planning to do for the party."

"Jessica," Elizabeth said sternly. "You didn't hear one word I said."

"Sure I did," Jessica assured her twin. "Janet

thinks that we should have pineapples hollowed out and filled with punch or fruit cup. She liked my suggestion that we have pineapple upside-down cake, too."

"She's all you talk about lately. Janet this and Janet that," Elizabeth said. "You're getting awfully boring, Jess."

"Thanks a lot!" Jessica snapped, her blue-green eyes flashing.

"But it's true, Jess. I hate to agree with Steven, but all we hear from you lately is *Janet says.*"

Jessica stood up and put both hands on her hips. "You're as bad as Lila. If you're getting jealous, just because I have an older friend—"

"You know better than that!" Elizabeth said. "I don't care who your friends are, Jessica. But spending time with Janet has really gone to your head. You think she's important just because she's an eighth grader. You'll be sorry if you drop all your other friends."

"See!" Jessica shook her blond hair. "I knew it. You're just jealous." She picked up another cookie and marched toward the front door. "I don't have to listen to you," she announced. "I'm going over to Janet's."

She slammed the door behind her and ran

down the front walk. She couldn't believe it! Her own twin was jealous of her new friendship. Well, Elizabeth and Lila would both be sorry. They would have to realize when Jessica and Janet turned out to be best friends that Jessica liked Janet for more than just her age. And could Jessica help it if Janet saw just how much fun she could be?

When Jessica reached the Howell's house, she hurried up the front walk to ring the doorbell. She heard the tinkling of the chimes and waited impatiently for someone to answer. The door opened, and Janet stood in the doorway. She looked surprised and not terribly pleased to see Jessica.

"Hi, Janet." Jessica sniffed. "Are the painters all finished? I don't smell any paint." She stared at the peach-colored wall behind Janet's head. There was no sign of workmen in the Howell residence.

For a moment Janet looked puzzled, then she shook her head. "No, they haven't started yet. They—uh—had to measure the dining room."

"I thought you said it was your kitchen that was being painted."

"That, too," Janet said. "But I still can't have any guests this week." She stepped outside and pulled the door shut behind her.

Jessica's heart sank. "Oh. Well, I thought we could talk awhile. You know, plan the party a little more, but if you can't—"

"I can come over to your house," Janet offered quickly.

"Oh, good," Jessica agreed. "We can talk there."

"Is your brother at home?" Janet asked Jessica as they walked down the sidewalk side by side.

"I doubt it," Jessica said. "So what do you think about making grass skirts for all the girls? It wouldn't be hard," she explained. "We could get some green crepe paper."

"I don't know," Janet said. "Grass skirts sound like a lot of trouble. What time do you think Steven will be home?"

"Who knows? And who cares?"

Jessica talked nonstop about her party plans, but Janet didn't seem very interested in her ideas. When they reached the Wakefield home and walked up the front drive, Janet became more attentive. "Is that your brother's bike?" she asked.

"Uh-huh," Jessica said impatiently. Why was Janet so interested in Steven, anyhow?

They entered the house, and Janet immediately headed for the kitchen. Jessica followed. "Want a snack?" she asked before she saw the empty cookie plate on the table. "Oh, no, the human vacuum cleaner has struck again."

Steven Wakefield sat at the table, munching on the last of the cookies.

"Really, Steven." Jessica glared at her brother. "You could have left some cookies for my company. Now there's nothing here for Janet."

"I didn't know you were having anyone over," Steven pointed out reasonably. "Sorry, Janet."

"Hi, Steven." Janet smiled at him. "That's OK. I wasn't hungry anyhow. How's school?"

"Fine," Steven said, washing down his last bite of cookie with a gulp of milk. He wiped his milky mustache away with the back of one hand.

"I hear you're the star of the junior varsity basketball team," Janet went on.

Jessica sniffed. "Don't encourage him," she warned. "That's all he ever talks about."

But Janet didn't listen. "I love basketball," she told Steven. "Tell me about practice. Is it fun?"

Steven didn't seem eager to answer. In fact, he looked a little uneasy as Janet continued to smile brightly at him. "Nothing much to tell. We just shoot baskets. Well, I'm sure you girls want to talk."

He stood up from the table, brushing cookie crumbs off his lap. "I'll go up to my room."

"Good." Jessica wanted to have her friend to herself.

"You don't have to leave," Janet protested.

While Jessica looked at Janet in surprise, Janet moved closer to Steven and put her hand on his arm. "Jessica and I were just discussing the big luau the Unicorns are going to host next week. Your parents agreed that we could have the party in your backyard. Of course we—the Unicorns, I mean—want you to come, Steven."

"Thanks, Janet, but I—uh, I already have plans," Steven said quickly.

Janet's smile faded. "I haven't even told you which night it's going to be!"

Steven looked guilty. "Well, you see, I'm really busy all next week," he explained. "Got to go."

He hurried out of the kitchen and raced up the stairs.

"What a pain! He just doesn't know a good thing when he sees it," Janet fumed.

Jessica stared at her. "Who cares if Steven comes to our party?" she demanded.

"What's the point of having it here if Steven doesn't come?" Janet answered, then bit her lip.

Jessica's eyes widened. "You mean that's why you wanted to hold the Unicorn party here?"

Janet didn't answer. She turned away from Jessica's accusing stare.

Jessica couldn't believe it. "You weren't interested in my ideas at all, were you, Janet? You just have a crush on my dumb brother. Of all the sneaky tricks to pull!"

Janet's face reddened. "What a thing to say, after I was nice enough to include you in the party planning! You should be pleased that I asked you. It's not every day I listen to a sixth grader's childish ideas."

"Childish?" Jessica sputtered. "I'm just as mature as you are, Janet Howell."

"That'll be the day!" Janet snapped.

"And my ideas are the best in the whole club," Jessica told her. "If you didn't have me to plan parties, the whole Unicorn Club would probably break up out of pure boredom."

"Ha, ha. That's what *you* think!" Janet threw back her head and laughed. "We'd get along just fine without you, Jessica Wakefield!"

"Maybe you should try, then." Jessica yelled. "Maybe I'll just resign from the Unicorns. Who needs such a sneaky bunch anyway!"

"See if I care!" Janet yelled back. She jumped up and stomped toward the door. "I'm going home."

"Good!" Jessica didn't even blink as Janet

slammed the door behind her. "If I resign," she shouted, hoping Janet could still hear her, "your whole club will probably fall apart!"

She ran to the phone to call Lila and tell her about the terrible trick Janet had pulled. But after she punched in the first number, she remembered that Lila was still mad at her.

"Oh, no," she said aloud. "Lila probably won't speak to me. Now Janet will ignore me, too. What am I going to do?"

Eight

Tuesday afternoon Sarah hurried home from school. Thank goodness Annie would be back tonight! Maybe she would get a good night's sleep.

By eight o'clock Annie still hadn't arrived, so Sarah turned the TV on and tried to watch one of her favorite comedy shows. *Annie's just late,* she told herself. *Annie's always late.*

She got up and switched on all the lights, then thought she heard the sound of a car in the driveway. She peered hopefully through the front window, but there was no sign of Annie's car.

It was way past the time Annie had promised to be back, and Sarah grew anxious and concerned.

Had Annie had an accident? Was she sick herself? What could have happened?

Sarah looked longingly at the telephone, but she didn't know whom to call. She had no way of reaching Annie, and she couldn't call her father because she'd have to tell him everything. Sarah couldn't decide what to do.

At eleven o'clock, she gave up hope and climbed into bed, but once again it was impossible to sleep.

On Wednesday morning Sarah pulled on her clothes without even washing up. She was too tired to care how she looked. She went through her morning classes in a fog. She didn't say a word to anybody. Even at lunch, she didn't say anything.

"Sarah," Elizabeth said, "we're talking about the history project. Aren't you listening?"

Sarah was too tired to even try and explain.

Elizabeth looked at Amy and shook her head. "I don't think she's heard a word."

But then she forgot about Sarah for a moment as Jessica approached her table with a lunch tray in hand.

"Hi, Lizzie. I really need to sit with you," Jessica said. Her face was red, and she sounded upset.

"Sure, Jess." Elizabeth motioned to the empty seat beside her. "Is something wrong?"

"I don't know what to do," Jessica moaned, putting her tray down beside her sister's. "I may really have to resign from the Unicorns after last night."

"That's too bad. I know how much you love the club."

"I do," Jessica admitted. "But Lila's still angry because I forgot about her last Saturday. She refused to come to the phone when I called her last night, and she still won't talk to me today. And Janet's still not talking to me, either."

Elizabeth giggled. "Janet has a crush on Steven," she explained to Amy.

"Can you believe it?" Jessica shook her head in disgust. "And when Steven turned down an invitation to our luau, Janet got really mad. She took it out on me, so I threatened to resign."

"I don't blame you for being angry, Jessica," Amy said.

Jessica poked at her coleslaw with her fork. "And now she's telling the rest of the club that my party plans are silly. If they agree, no one will care if I resign!" Jessica sighed.

Elizabeth looked up and saw Sarah take her tray to the counter and wander into the hall.

"Lizzie," Jessica continued, "what am I going to do?"

* * *

Sarah made her way to math class and sank into her seat. She tried to listen to Ms. Wyler, but the writing on the blackboard seemed to run together, and her eyes just wouldn't stay open. The teacher's voice seemed far away.

"Sarah!"

Sarah jerked, lifting her head off the desk. The teacher's sharp tone forced her momentarily awake. "I'm here—I mean, what did you say?" she stammered. To Sarah's alarm, she saw Ms. Wyler approach her desk. The teacher was frowning.

"This is not the time for a nap!"

"I'm sorry," Sarah murmured, feeling herself blushing as the rest of the class stared.

"Are you feeling ill, Sarah?"

Sarah longed to say yes, knowing that Ms. Wyler's annoyed expression would soften. But then she would be sent to the nurse's office. She just couldn't risk it.

"No, Ms. Wyler." Sarah struggled to look awake. But her eyelids were very heavy, and she felt a yawn coming on. She shut her mouth firmly and tried to hold it back but succeeded only in forming a strange expression.

Ms. Wyler seemed to think Sarah was trying to

clown. "This is no time for joking, Sarah," she said. "I think you'd better try to pay attention. Your work this week has hardly been satisfactory."

"Yes, Ms. Wyler," Sarah answered. Several of her classmates stared at her curiously. Sarah wished she could sink through the floor.

The teacher walked back to the front of the room and continued with the lesson. Sarah tried her best to stay awake, but she felt her head drooping again.

"Sarah?" The whisper came from beside her. She started. She looked across the aisle at Elizabeth Wakefield. "Is anything wrong?" Elizabeth asked.

Sarah shook her head. "No," she whispered back. "Nothing special."

If only she could tell Elizabeth the truth. But that was impossible!

Nine

◇

When Sarah reached home on Wednesday afternoon, she suddenly remembered that she had promised to meet Elizabeth and Amy after school. Or was
that yesterday they had planned to meet? Two nights
of little sleep had affected her memory. Sarah's head
felt like it was stuffed with cotton.

The house echoed with emptiness. Too ex-
hausted to climb the stairs to her room, Sarah
dropped her schoolbooks and jacket in the middle of
the hall floor and sank down on the living room sofa.
Putting her head down on a cushion, she thought,
I'll just rest a minute.

The next thing she heard was the jangling of the

phone. Her mind blurred with sleep, she jumped up so quickly that the sudden movement made her head spin. Steadying herself, she ran for the phone.

"Annie?" she gasped. "Is that you?"

After a long silence, a familiar voice spoke sharply. "Sarah? It's Aunt Lillian. Is something wrong?"

"No, no," Sarah sputtered, alarmed that she'd said the wrong thing. "I just thought—uh, Annie usually calls in the afternoon."

"Are you sure nothing's wrong?"

"Positive, Aunt Lillian." Sarah swallowed hard. She hated lying. If only Annie would come back. Then everything would go back to normal.

"Is your father home?"

"No, he hasn't come home from work yet," Sarah said. At least that was true, in a way.

"How's school, dear?" her aunt asked.

"Fine," Sarah said, trying to sound sincere. Even that was a lie. She tried to think of something truthful to say.

"I'm working on a history project with Elizabeth and Amy, two of my friends from school," she told her aunt. She didn't have to tell her aunt that Elizabeth and Amy had done most of the work so far.

They talked for a few more minutes, then her

aunt said goodbye. Sarah hung up the phone. She looked at the clock on the wall. Where was Annie? Wasn't she ever coming back?

It was almost time for dinner, but Sarah wasn't hungry. She walked into the kitchen and opened a cabinet door, but nothing appealed to her. She was tired of canned food. She walked over to the refriger-ator and peered into the freezer. There was a small frozen pizza, but even that didn't tempt her. Maybe later.

She picked up her books and jacket and climbed the stairs. Dumping her belongings on her bed, she went to the bathroom to turn on the water. The night before she'd even been too tired to take a bath, and now she felt she needed one.

She locked the bathroom door before she stepped into the tub, aware of the big empty house all around her. She'd hardly settled into the warm water before a creaking sound in the attic made her jump.

Sarah grabbed her washcloth and scrubbed her arms. She was determined to ignore the slight set-tling noises of the old house.

But a sudden sharp sound made her nervous all over again. "Oh, no! It's the phone!" Sarah shrieked. "I'm coming, I'm coming."

Sarah shivered as the cool air met her wet skin. She quickly dried off and ran to the phone, but by the time she got to it, it had stopped ringing. The slight buzz of the dial tone was her only answer.

"Hello, hello?" Sarah repeated, her voice forlorn. This was terrible! Who had it been? Annie? Her father?

She sniffed as she replaced the receiver and walked back to the bathroom, trying not to cry. Her bathwater was cold. She let the water out and got into her pajamas. She was just hanging her towel on the rack when the phone rang again.

This time Sarah raced for it, scrambling straight across her father's big bed.

"Hello?" she gasped. "Who is it?"

"It's me, Annie. Who'd you expect?"

Sarah was so happy to hear the woman's voice that she ignored the sarcasm. "Annie? Where have you been? When are you coming home? I was so worried."

"Worried? What were you worried about?" Annie sounded annoyed. Sarah couldn't seem to do anything right when it came to Annie.

Sarah didn't want to argue, though. She only wanted Annie, grumpy or not, to come back. She didn't think she could bear another night alone in the big house. "I'm sorry," she apologized hurriedly. "Are you coming home soon?"

"I can't come yet," Annie said, speaking very quickly. "My little sister's still not feeling well. It looks like I'll have to stay here till Saturday."

"Saturday!" Sarah was sure her heart had stopped. "I can't stay by myself that long."

She began to cry, quietly at first, then louder and louder, no longer able to pretend.

"Come on, don't be such a baby," Annie snapped. "You might try thinking about *me* for a change."

But even the nasty edge to Annie's voice couldn't slow Sarah's tears. "But Annie," Sarah sobbed, "I'm so scared when I'm here all by myself."

"Now listen to me, Sarah," Annie commanded. "When I was your age, I stayed alone all the time. I had to take care of all my little brothers and sisters after my parents died. I was even younger than you are, in fact. I didn't moan and groan and feel sorry for myself. You should be ashamed, a big girl like you!"

Sarah tried hard to swallow her sobs. She wanted to act like a twelve-year-old, not a baby.

"I'm sorry," she said, feeling miserable all over again. "I'm just scared, Annie."

"Well, don't worry so much," Annie told her. "This is good for you. It will help you become more grown-up, you know."

Sarah didn't want to be grown-up yet. "What about the rest of your family?" she asked timidly. "Isn't there anyone else who can stay with your little sister?"

"If someone else could do it," Annie answered, "do you think I'd be here? Now stop making such a fuss."

"I'll try." Sarah sighed.

"And don't forget what we agreed about your father. We don't want to worry him for no reason," Annie continued.

"I won't," Sarah promised.

She hung up the phone, unable to suppress another loud sob. How on earth could she manage till Saturday? She was already a nervous wreck. She wiped her cheeks with the back of her hand and tried to think. Wandering over to the big desk in the corner of the room, she ran her palm over the smooth oak surface. The desk had once held her mother's books and papers. But Annie had put all the books away. "A bunch of junk," Sarah had heard her say. She had replaced the books with her makeup and nail polish.

Sarah had once remarked to her father that Annie wasn't much like her mother. Mr. Thomas had turned red and seemed offended at the comment.

"Your mother graduated from UCLA with honors," he explained. "Before she got sick, she was planning to go back to school and earn her master's degree. It's different for Annie. She never got to attend college; she was too busy raising her little brothers and sisters after her parents died. You know that, Sarah."

Sarah felt guilty, and she never brought the subject up again. But looking down now at the mess Annie had made of her mother's beautiful desk, Sarah thought she would burst into tears again.

If Annie had worked hard as a child, why did she work so little now? Sarah just didn't understand it.

The thought of two more lonely nights in this big old house was truly awful. Then she remembered Elizabeth and Amy. They were supposed to sleep over on Friday night. She'd have to tell them not to come. *I can't let anyone find out that I'm all alone.*

Was it too late to call them? Sarah glanced at the clock on her father's bedside table and ran back to the phone. She dialed Amy's number first. Mrs. Sutton answered.

"Is Amy there?" Sarah asked timidly.

"I'm sorry, dear, she's in bed." Mrs. Sutton said. "May I give her a message?"

"Yes, please tell her that Sarah called, and I won't be able to have her sleep over on Friday," Sarah said quickly. "Tell her I'm sorry."

She said goodbye and hung up, relieved. That was one call taken care of. She dialed the Wakefield home next.

"Hello?"

"Hi, Elizabeth. This is Sarah."

"Hi, Sarah. What's up?" Elizabeth asked.

"Elizabeth, I'm sorry, but I can't have you and Amy sleep over on Friday night."

"That's too bad," Elizabeth said. "Aside from the school project, it would have been fun."

"I know," Sarah agreed. "I'm sorry."

"That's OK." Elizabeth was quiet for a moment. "You're not sick, are you, Sarah?"

"No," Sarah mumbled.

"Then would you like to sleep over my house Friday night instead?" Elizabeth asked. "I know it will be all right with my parents for you and Amy to spend the night."

"Really?" Sarah said. She was relieved and excited.

"Sure," Elizabeth told her. "Why don't we plan on it?"

"That would be great." Sarah smiled for the first time all week. "Thanks, Elizabeth."

When she hung up, she felt a little better. Just two more nights alone. Then she could go to Elizabeth's.

Ten

◇

"What an awful week this has been," Jessica said as she and Elizabeth walked to school. "I'm so glad it's Friday."

Elizabeth looked closely at her twin. She certainly wasn't acting like her usual bubbly self. "Didn't you and Lila make up yet?"

Jessica gave an exaggerated sigh. "No, and today there's a Unicorn meeting after school."

"That should give you a chance to clear things up with Janet and Lila."

"But it won't, Lizzie." Jessica cried. "What if I have to resign? I'll just die. I can't imagine not being a Unicorn."

To Elizabeth, not being a Unicorn didn't seem the worst of all possible fates. But one quick glance at Jessica and she knew that her sister was very upset. She looked as if she might cry.

"Don't worry, Jess," Elizabeth said. "I'm sure they don't want to lose you. You're great at parties and—organizing activities and—well, lots of fun things."

Jessica nodded but still looked unhappy. "But I'm the one who said I might resign," she reminded her twin. "What if Janet expects me to follow through?"

"Janet must know you didn't really mean it, Jess."

"I don't know," Jessica said. "You didn't see how angry she was the other day. I'm afraid she'll try to convince everyone to drop me. I heard her talking to the other Unicorns about my ideas for the party, trying to tell them my plans weren't any good."

"That doesn't mean they'll listen," Elizabeth pointed out.

"But Janet's so popular. *Everyone* listens to her!"

Elizabeth shook her head. It was obvious nothing was going to make Jessica feel any better right now. "I hope it turns out OK, Jess. But you know you're still *my* best friend, whatever happens."

"That won't help if I can't be a Unicorn anymore," Jessica said.

Elizabeth didn't know whether to be angry or amused. It was just like Jessica not to consider her feelings. But she could never stay annoyed at her twin for long. "Thanks, Jess," she managed to say through her laughter.

Jessica look guilty. "Oh, Lizzie, I didn't mean that the way it sounded. You know I care a lot about you. It's just that being a Unicorn is so important to me!"

Elizabeth nodded. "I understand."

Jessica gave her twin an impulsive hug. "Thanks, Lizzie."

"Good luck," Elizabeth said as they neared the school.

"Thanks, I'm going to need it!" She marched up the front steps, looking determined. At the end of the first hallway, she located Lila.

"Don't say a word!" Jessica declared. "I've got something to say to you, Lila."

Lila waited, her brows arching in surprise.

"I'm sorry I hurt your feelings last Saturday," Jessica announced. "You're my friend, and I don't want you to be angry at me."

Staring anxiously at Lila, Jessica waited for her reaction. To her relief, Lila grinned.

"That's OK, Jess," she said. "I was getting tired of being mad. I missed you this week."

"You did?" Jessica exhaled loudly. She already felt better. "Well, I should hope so!"

They both giggled. Lila linked her arm through Jessica's, and the two girls walked down the hall, chattering about that afternoon's Unicorn meeting.

Jessica tensed at the thought of the meeting. Lila was her friend again. But what about Janet and the rest of the Unicorns? Would Jessica be forced to resign? After all, the president of the club was certainly the most influential member.

Elizabeth found Amy Sutton in front of her locker. Amy waited while Elizabeth collected her books, then the two friends walked toward their first class.

"Look, there's Sarah," Amy observed. "She looks terrible."

Sarah had dark circles under her eyes, and her skin was pale. Her hair looked as if it hadn't been combed in days, and her clothes seemed to have been thrown on hastily. The bottom button on her blouse wasn't buttoned, and her jeans were slightly wrinkled.

"She looks as if she got dressed in her sleep," Amy said. "Do you think she's sick?"

"She hasn't looked right all week," Elizabeth said. "But if she's ill, why doesn't she stay home?"

"Beats me," Amy said. "If I looked like that, my mom would send me straight to bed. Why don't her parents—oh, I forgot. Sarah only has her dad."

"And Annie," Elizabeth noted.

"Who's Annie?" Amy sounded curious.

Elizabeth shook her head. "It's a long story. Sarah!" she called.

Sarah turned around and gave Elizabeth and Amy a limp wave. The girls walked across the hall to meet her.

"Hi, Sarah. How are you?" Elizabeth asked.

"I'm OK," Sarah said.

"You don't look OK," Amy said bluntly.

"Amy's right, Sarah. Maybe you should go to the nurse's office," Elizabeth suggested.

"No, no," Sarah said quickly, her eyes filling with tears. "I can't, I mean, I don't want to. I'm OK, really. Just leave me alone."

She hurried away, leaving the other two girls to

stare after her. Amy shrugged. "I don't understand what's going on."

Elizabeth shook her head. "Me, neither. But, maybe she'll confide in us tonight at the sleep-over."

At the sound of the final bell, the two girls headed for their classrooms.

At three o'clock, Jessica and Lila rushed out the front door of the school. "Hooray for Friday," Lila said. "Hey, Jess, there are the rest of the Unicorns. They're waiting for us."

Jessica gulped. *At least Lila is on my side,* she reminded herself. The two girls walked toward the fountain in front of the school where the rest of their club, including Janet, had gathered. Jessica tried to smile confidently, as if she were sure of her welcome. She would never let Janet know that her stomach was full of butterflies.

"Hi, Lila. Hi, Jessica," Tamara Chase called. "We're all going over to Janet's to talk about the big luau."

"What, no painters?" Jessica muttered under her breath.

"Hey, Jess," Ellen Riteman said. "Janet told us about your ideas for the party."

Jessica braced herself, waiting for a storm of criticism.

"We love it," Betsy Gordon told her. "A poolside luau, Hawaiian music—"

"And grass skirts," Kimberly Haver exclaimed.

Jessica tried to hide her surprise. "You mean you don't think it's too much work?"

"Not at all. It'll be the best party the Unicorns have ever had," Kimberly assured her.

"Well, I knew it was a good idea," Jessica said, smiling broadly.

"You always have the best ideas," Ellen said.

"Just wait," Lila said, linking arms with Jessica. "Jessica and I will coordinate the whole party."

They began to discuss the details as they walked in one big noisy group toward Janet's house. Only Janet Howell herself remained silent.

She must still be mad, Jessica thought.

But before they reached Camden Drive, Janet managed to fall into step beside Jessica. She leaned close and spoke quietly into her ear.

"Jessica, I—well, I didn't mean what I said the other day. I think your idea is great."

"Oh, thanks, Janet," Jessica said lightly, as if she'd never doubted it at all.

Janet hesitated, then added, "If Steven changes

his mind, tell him he's still invited." She looked hopefully at Jessica.

Jessica tried not to giggle. "I'll tell him."

Lila, eyeing them with curiosity, hurried Jessica away from Janet. "Anything I should know about?" she asked.

Jessica grinned. "We were just agreeing on what a good idea the luau is," she said. What a relief it was to know she wouldn't have to resign from the club after all.

Eleven

◇

This Friday afternoon Sarah's walk home seemed to last forever. She was so weary she could hardly stand up. The last few days had passed like a dark dream, and now, at last, the school week was over.

When her house finally came into view, Sarah sighed and pulled out her key. She looked wistfully at the driveway, hoping for the sight of Annie's car, or better yet, her father's. But the driveway was empty.

She unlocked the door and let herself in. She had almost forgotten how bright and cheerful coming home used to be. Now the house was too big and dreary, even though it was a sunny afternoon. The sounds she made when she set her books on the table and shut the front door seemed to echo through the house.

She walked into the kitchen, but she felt too nervous to eat. Her stomach quivered and knotted at every sound. Thank goodness she would be going to Elizabeth's house in a few hours. And the next day Annie would be back, and finally, on Sunday, her father would return. It was hard to believe he had only been gone one week. It felt like an eternity.

Sarah decided to go up to her room and pack her bag for her sleepover at Elizabeth's house. As she started up the stairs, she glanced at the pile of schoolbooks on the hall table. She was too tired to do any schoolwork now, so she chose to leave them there.

After packing her bag, Sarah glanced at her desk clock and decided to wait in her room until it was time for Elizabeth to pick her up. She felt more secure there.

She picked up her old teddy bear and hugged it, then perched anxiously on the side of her bed to watch the clock. Elizabeth and Amy would be there soon.

Bang! A sudden sharp noise from the lower floor sent Sarah flying to her feet. She screamed.

It was *not* one of the usual creaks or shudders

that the house made. Something—or someone—had made that loud noise! Was there an intruder? She would have to go look. She couldn't just wait in her room for whomever it was to find her.

She dropped her stuffed bear and ran out to the hall. As she scrambled down the steps, her feet seemed to tangle themselves into a giant knot. Crying out in alarm, Sarah plummeted wildly down the stairs.

"Ouch!" she cried, as the wood banister struck her forehead. The pain brought tears to her eyes. She continued to roll down the stairs. She collapsed at the bottom, landing heavily on her right foot.

Everything hurt her, and she cried harder than she had ever cried before. She laid her head against the bottom step and sobbed. She felt miserable.

Across the hallway, Sarah noticed her schoolbooks lying on the floor. They must have fallen off the table. That was the loud noise that she had heard. If she hadn't hurt herself, it would have been funny, but right now Sarah couldn't muster a smile.

If only she could call someone. But the phone seemed miles away, and she couldn't stand up.

She tried to raise her head, but the whole house spun around her.

"Oh, Dad," she murmured. "Where are you?"

Twelve

◇

After supper on Friday evening, Elizabeth dragged her father out to the garage and jumped into their maroon van.

"You seem pretty excited, sweetheart. All ready to go?" Mr. Wakefield asked.

"Ready! Amy first," Elizabeth said.

When they pulled up at Amy's house, Amy was waiting in the driveway. She waved goodbye to her mother, then climbed in.

"On to Sarah's house," Elizabeth told her father.

A few minutes later, the van turned into the Thomases' wide driveway.

"Is this the right place?" she asked Amy.

Amy nodded. "I gave Sarah a ride to a birthday party once. But I don't see her. I thought she'd be waiting outside for us."

"Maybe she forgot what time we were coming," Elizabeth said. "I'll go ring the doorbell."

She slipped out of the van and ran up the front drive. Silvery chimes sounded inside the house when she pushed the bell. She waited, expecting to hear footsteps as someone came to answer the door. But there was no sound at all.

She walked back to the van, feeling puzzled and a little worried. "I don't understand," she told her father. "No one answered."

"Could she have changed her mind about spending the night?" Mr. Wakefield asked.

Elizabeth shook her head. "I'm sure that if Sarah had decided not to come, she'd have called me."

"Hey, look, Elizabeth. There's a light on upstairs. Someone must be home," Amy said.

"I'm going to try the doorbell again," Elizabeth announced.

Mr. Wakefield turned off the engine. "I'll come with you," he said.

Amy jumped out and hurried after them. Elizabeth pushed the doorbell once more, and they all heard the sound of the chimes. Still nothing stirred inside the house.

"I just know something's wrong," Elizabeth said. She had to get a glimpse inside the house.

She took a giant step over some small shrubs to peer through the small window beside the door. She put her face close to the glass, her hands against the pane to shield her eyes from the reflection. What she saw inside the dark hall made her gasp.

"Dad!" she cried. "Come look!"

Mr. Wakefield stepped over the bushes and peered inside the window. Amy, too curious to wait, hurried up beside him. She shrieked when she saw the huddled body at the foot of the stairs.

"It's Sarah!" Amy cried.

Elizabeth's heart was pounding. She could hardly breathe. Amy ran to try the front door, only to find that it was locked.

"We don't have any time to waste. I'll have to break the glass." Mr. Wakefield announced. He grabbed a rock from under a bush and gave the windowpane one sharp tap. It shattered. Then he carefully removed several large pieces of glass and reached through to unlock the window. He raised himself above the empty frame and tried to squeeze his upper body through. It was too narrow for his broad shoulders.

"Let me try, Dad," Elizabeth urged. "I'm smaller than you."

"I don't know, Elizabeth. There's glass all over the floor. I don't want you to get hurt."

"I'll be careful. We have to get Sarah," Elizabeth said.

"You're right," Mr. Wakefield agreed. He lifted Elizabeth so she could slide easily through the narrow opening.

Elizabeth slipped to the floor and stepped carefully over the glass shards. Then she ran to Sarah's motionless body. She leaned over and touched her friend cautiously.

"She's breathing!" Elizabeth cried out.

"Unlock the door," Mr. Wakefield called.

Elizabeth ran back to the front door and turned the lock. Mr. Wakefield came in with Amy right behind him. They all bent over Sarah. Mr. Wakefield touched her wrist gently, feeling for a pulse. Then he went to the phone in the kitchen and dialed the emergency number.

"Hello," he said as soon as someone answered. "We need an ambulance." While he gave the details to the police dispatcher on the phone, Elizabeth and Amy knelt beside Sarah's still body.

Mr. Wakefield hung up the phone and came

back to the hallway. "The ambulance is on the way," he said. "I don't understand where her parents are."

"She lives alone with her father," Amy explained. "Her mother died when she was little."

"Well, do either of you know where Mr. Thomas works?" Mr. Wakefield asked. "What's the name of his company?"

Elizabeth and Amy looked at each other, their faces blank. "He has something to do with a clothing company, but I don't know the name," Elizabeth told her father.

"Aha," Mr. Wakefield said. He pointed to a small brass plaque on the wall in the foyer. "With appreciation to Robert Howard Thomas," it said. "For fifteen years with Trim Fit Clothes."

Mr. Wakefield went back to the phone and dialed information. By the time the girls heard the shrill sound of the ambulance siren, Mr. Wakefield had reached a security guard at the clothing company.

"Dad, they're here," Elizabeth called. She ran to open the door and let the uniformed paramedic inside. He hurried to kneel beside Sarah's body. Then he carefully checked her pulse, her heartbeat and her blood pressure while Elizabeth and Amy watched anxiously.

Another man appeared in the doorway, and the first medic called out, "Bring in the stretcher, Harry."

Very carefully, the two men placed Sarah on the stretcher and carried her back to the red-and-white van.

"Are you her father?" the first medic asked Mr. Wakefield, as he strapped the stretcher into the back of the ambulance. "We need a consent form signed."

"No," Mr. Wakefield said. "Her father is in Texas. I've called his company, and they're getting in touch with him. I'm sure he'll get here as soon as he possibly can. She can't have been staying alone. Girls, do you know any others in the family?"

Elizabeth and Amy both shook their heads. "There's her father's fiancée, Annie," Elizabeth told her dad. "But I don't think she lives here."

Mr. Wakefield frowned. "We'll leave a note here in case someone returns. Right now, I'll drop you girls at home and go on to the hospital."

Elizabeth's eyes widened, and Amy looked alarmed. "Take us with you, Daddy," Elizabeth begged. "We have to know if Sarah is going to be all right."

Thirteen

◇

Elizabeth and Amy sat side by side in the Emergency Room waiting area. Mr. Wakefield went down the hall to call Mrs. Wakefield and tell her what had happened. When he returned, they all waited anxiously.

At last a doctor in green coveralls came to find them. "You're with the little girl who just came in?" he asked.

Mr. Wakefield nodded.

Elizabeth sat up straight and Amy bit her nails.

"How is she?" Mr. Wakefield asked.

"Will she be all right?" Elizabeth blurted.

The doctor's expression was somber. "I hope so," he said. "Your friend received some cuts and bruises from her fall, and two small bones are bro-ken in her foot, but her concussion is the most seri-ous problem."

"How bad is it?" Mr. Wakefield asked.

"We'll just have to wait and see. Right now all we know is that there's no skull fracture. That's a good sign, but I'm afraid she hasn't regained con-sciousness yet."

While the two men talked quietly, Elizabeth looked at Amy. "She's got to be OK," she whispered.

When the doctor left, Mr. Wakefield turned back to the girls. "I'd better take you home," he told them. "All we can do now is wait."

"No, Dad," Elizabeth said. "We can't leave Sarah here all alone. We have to stay."

"It may be hours before Sarah wakes," Mr. Wakefield said. "There's nothing we can do for her right now, and it's very late."

"I just know I wouldn't sleep, Daddy," Eliza-beth told him. "What if Sarah wakes up and there's no one here that she knows! She'll be so frightened! Please, Dad. What if it were me, all alone?"

Mr. Wakefield reached out and hugged Eliza-beth, then put one arm around Amy and drew her close. "You're both very considerate girls," he told them. "You're right. It would be bad if Sarah woke up and didn't see a familiar face. I guess it wouldn't be terrible if you lost one night's sleep."

"Thank you, Daddy." Elizabeth hugged her father.

"I'm going to call your mother again," Mr. Wakefield said. "She'll want to hear about Sarah's condition. And I'll tell her that we're staying."

Elizabeth sat on a waiting-room couch and stared through the cream-colored blinds into the dark night. *Oh, Sarah*, she thought. *Please be OK.*

She was sure she was too worried to be tired. But the window blinds began to blur, and her head drooped. The next thing she heard was the sound of cars honking on the street outside. She blinked hard at the daylight coming through the window. It was morning. Her neck ached and her whole body felt stiff. She looked at Amy, sprawled across the other end of the couch. She was still asleep, her hair strewn across her face. Mr. Wakefield was dozing in a chair across the room.

Suddenly Elizabeth heard the sound of a man's voice coming from the nurse's station down the hall. He sounded very upset.

"Is my daughter here—Sarah Thomas? How is she?"

"Dad!" Elizabeth said, "Sarah's father is here."

Mr. Wakefield awoke with a jolt and hurried over to the nurse's station. Elizabeth heard him speak quietly to Mr. Thomas, then both men walked back to the waiting area.

"She's still unconscious," Mr. Thomas told them. He looked tired and worried, and his suit was rumpled from his overnight flight. "I can't understand what happened. How was she hurt? Did someone break into the house?" He looked around the waiting room. "Hasn't Annie been here with you?"

Mr. Wakefield tried to explain. "We found Sarah unconscious when I drove the girls over to pick her up for a sleep-over. She must have fallen down the stairs. I had to break a windowpane to get in. There was no one else in the house."

Mr. Thomas put one hand to his head. "How could this have happened? Are you sure Annie isn't hurt, too?"

"I walked through the house before I came to the hospital. I'm sure no one else was there." Mr. Wakefield sounded firm.

Mr. Thomas looked bewildered. He sat down and covered his face with his hands. "I don't understand," he said over and over. "My poor baby. What would have happened if you hadn't shown up? How can I ever thank you?"

"It was Elizabeth who insisted we investigate when no one answered the door," Mr. Wakefield told him.

Mr. Thomas looked at Elizabeth. His eyes were red and puffy. It looked as if he had been crying. "Thank you, Elizabeth," he said. "Sarah's lucky to have you as a friend."

Elizabeth's eyes filled with tears. She had to swallow hard. Mr. Thomas held out his hand, and she shook it solemnly.

The sound of the nurse's voice made them all turn. "Mr. Thomas?" she said. "I think Sarah's coming around."

Mr. Thomas hurried down the hall after the nurse. Mr. Wakefield followed. Elizabeth looked at Amy.

"Do you think they'll let us in?" Amy said.

"Maybe we could just peek," Elizabeth suggested. The girls ran after the two men.

The nurse was so busy checking Sarah's pulse that she didn't notice the girls peering around the doorway. They saw Sarah blink and turn her head.

"Daddy?" she murmured. "Is that you? My head hurts, Daddy."

"Sarah!" Mr. Thomas cried with emotion.

"Thank goodness. You're going to be OK, sweetheart." He stroked her arm.

Sarah clung to his hand. "I'm so glad you're home," she said, her voice weak. "I was so scared all alone."

"Why were you alone, Sarah?" Mr. Thomas bent lower, trying to hear her words. "Where was Annie?"

Watching from the doorway, Elizabeth saw Sarah's expression change. "I can't tell." Sarah started to cry. "I promised."

"It's all right, Sarah," her father said quickly. "You can tell me anything."

"Annie had to go," Sarah said softly. "Her little sister got sick."

"When did she leave?"

"On Monday," Sarah told him.

"Monday!" Mr. Thomas sounded alarmed. "But why did she—why on earth—" he stammered.

The nurse waved him away from the bed. "No more talking now," she said. "We don't want to tire her out. You can speak to your daughter again a little bit later."

Elizabeth scooted back into the hallway before the nurse saw her. Amy followed, and they all walked back to the waiting room.

Mr. Thomas looked relieved but still puzzled. "I

have to find out where my fiancée is," he told them. "I'm going to make a call."

He looked through his wallet and pulled out a small piece of paper with a phone number written on it. He crossed to the pay phone on the opposite wall and picked up the receiver.

"Time for us to go, girls," Mr. Wakefield said. "Sarah will be all right now that her father's here."

"When will she be able to go home?" Elizabeth asked.

"I'm not sure."

As the girls walked over to the couch to get their jackets, they couldn't help overhearing Mr. Thomas on the phone.

"Hello," he said. "Is Annie Jo Mapleton there?" After a pause, he frowned. "She's not? I understood that her younger sister was taken ill. What do you mean, she doesn't have a younger sister?"

Amy looked at Elizabeth, wide-eyed. Then they looked back at Mr. Thomas. His expression had changed from concern to anger. "She hasn't been home at all?"

He listened another minute, then hung up the phone.

Elizabeth put her jacket on slowly, hoping Mr. Thomas would tell them what had happened. But he never had a chance to explain. Just then a young woman with a stylish hairdo and a short, tight skirt rushed through the doorway.

"Robbie," she cried. "I found a note at home that said—I can explain. It wasn't my fault!" She threw her arms around him.

Mr. Thomas took a step back. "Annie, where have you been?"

"My little sister was very ill. I had to rush back home to take care of her. Sarah told me she didn't mind staying alone for just . . ." Annie's voice trailed off under Mr. Thomas's angry glare.

"Everything you've told me about your family is a lie," he said. "I just called your sister's home. She said you haven't been there in weeks. You don't even *have* a baby sister, she told me. You're the youngest in your family, Annie. And all you can do is make excuses. You haven't even bothered to ask how Sarah is."

"Oh, well, I was just about to ask," Annie said. "You didn't give me a chance. You never think about me at all, Robbie."

Elizabeth watched Annie stamp her feet. She sounded just like Jessica having a tantrum.

"I didn't realize how much you need to grow up yourself, Annie," Mr. Thomas said. "I've been very blind. I should never have left Sarah alone with you."

Annie tossed her head back. "Don't you think I have the right to have a little fun?"

Mr. Thomas's voice hardened. "How can you think about yourself at a time like this, Annie? Sarah could have died, thanks to you. You could have at least called a neighbor to stay with her." Mr. Thomas shook his head. "There's no excuse for this, Annie."

"If that's the way you feel," Annie yelled, "I don't think you love me at all. Maybe I should just leave!"

"Maybe you should," Mr. Thomas said quietly.

Annie looked surprised, then outraged. Then, without another word, she stomped away.

Elizabeth sighed with relief, remembering what Sarah had told her about Annie. "Everything's going to be great now," she whispered to Amy.

"Let's go, girls," Mr. Wakefield said. "You've had enough time to eavesdrop."

Blushing, Elizabeth followed her father out to the hall. "We'll call later to see how Sarah is," Mr. Wakefield told Mr. Thomas.

Elizabeth almost bumped into a dark-haired woman who was hurrying down the hallway.

"Lillian?" Mr. Thomas looked shocked. "What are you doing here?"

"What's happened to Sarah?" the woman demanded. "I let myself into the house and found a note—saying Sarah was in the hospital. Is she all right?"

"She has a concussion, but she seems to be doing well," Mr. Thomas assured her. "But what are you doing in Sweet Valley?"

Elizabeth watched them as she waited for the elevator with Amy and her father. The woman looked angry and upset. She took a deep breath before she answered.

"I spoke to Sarah this week and she sounded terrible. I could tell something was wrong but she wouldn't tell me what it was. I finally tried to call you at work, and they told me you were in Texas! You didn't leave Sarah all alone, did you?"

"Of course not." Mr. Thomas looked embarrassed. "I thought Annie was there with her, but she left—"

"I knew it!" Lillian said. "This is unforgivable, Robert! You don't deserve a darling child like Sarah if you can't take proper care of her. She'd be better off living with me."

Mr. Thomas looked shocked.

Elizabeth turned to Amy. "Oh, no," she murmured. "What's going to happen to Sarah now?"

Fourteen

◇

Sarah sat on her bed at home, propped up with extra pillows as she ate a bowl of ice cream.

"Sarah," Aunt Lillian called from downstairs, "you have a visitor."

"Oh, good," Sarah said. She was awfully tired of being stuck in bed. "Who is it?"

"Me." Elizabeth Wakefield walked into the bedroom. "I came straight over after school. Everyone is asking about you. How do you feel?"

"Oh, Elizabeth!" Sarah smiled at her friend. "Thank you for everything. You saved my life!"

Elizabeth blushed. "How's your foot?" She glanced at the cast on Sarah's right foot. "I thought ice cream was for patients who'd had their tonsils out," Elizabeth teased.

Sarah grinned. "Ice cream is good for anything," she said.

Elizabeth giggled. "Was your dad angry at you when you finally told him the truth about Annie?" she asked.

Sarah shook her head vigorously. "No, not at all. He told me I should have talked to him a long time ago. He apologized for neglecting me and promised it would never happen again."

"That's great, Sarah. Aren't you happy now?"

"I would be," Sarah confessed. "But Aunt Lillian's still angry at my dad. She wants me to come live with her."

Elizabeth looked alarmed. "You mean leave Sweet Valley? Do you want to go?"

Sarah shook her head. "I love Aunt Lillian, and I love to visit her in the summer. But I want to live with my dad." Sarah's eyes filled with tears and she had to blink hard.

"Have you told your aunt that?" Elizabeth asked.

"No," Sarah admitted. "I don't want to hurt her feelings."

"I don't think you will. She's only concerned about you," Elizabeth told Sarah. "You have to be honest with her. Look what happened because you were afraid to talk to your dad!"

Sarah bit her lip. "I never thought of it like that," she admitted. "You're right, Elizabeth. I'll tell her how I feel."

"Good," Elizabeth said. "I'll go now, so you can have a chance to talk to her. But let me know what happens. Oh, and Sarah, I almost forgot. Do you think you'll be well enough to come to our luau on Saturday night?"

"I think so," Sarah said. "A party sounds like fun. I won't be able to dance, but I can sit by the pool."

"Great," Elizabeth said. "We want you to be the guest of honor!"

"You mean it?" Sarah grinned.

Elizabeth nodded. "Even Jessica and the Unicorns agreed. "They think your accident was very exciting," she said with a grin. "Besides, they want to hear all the details."

Both girls giggled.

"I'll call you later," Sarah promised.

*　　*　　*

Elizabeth walked home, happy that things had turned out so well for Sarah. She was sure her Aunt Lillian would understand.

"Sarah looks almost as good as new," Elizabeth told her mother and Jessica when she found them in the kitchen. Jessica was talking on the phone. "I told her we hoped she could come to the party. I just hope it doesn't turn out to be a farewell party for her."

"Why? Is Mr. Thomas moving?" Mrs. Wakefield asked.

"No. It's sort of complicated." Elizabeth looked at her sister. "I'm waiting for Sarah to call," she told her twin. "Can't you get off the phone for a while?"

Jessica frowned, but she said goodbye and hung up.

"Lila was telling me all the latest gossip, Lizzie. Did you know Ellen Riteman just got a new horse?" she said. "A beautiful Arabian named Snow White. And did you hear that Mrs. Waldron is having her niece, Ginny Lu, come and stay with her? She comes from Tennessee. She probably lives on some mountaintop in the middle of nowhere. Boy, will she be impressed with Sweet Valley. I bet she's never even seen a television!"

The phone rang before Elizabeth could answer.

"I'll get it," she yelled. Running across the room, she managed, for once, to beat Jessica to the phone.

"Hello? Hi, Sarah. I was hoping it was you," Elizabeth said. She listened intently for a few moments, then hung up the phone and grinned.

"Well?" Jessica demanded. "What happened?" Does she have to leave Sweet Valley?"

"No, everything worked out fine. Her aunt understands," Elizabeth answered.

"Good," Mrs. Wakefield said. "I hope Sarah can relax and get well now."

"She will," Elizabeth beamed. "And our luau will be a great way to celebrate."

"Don't forget, *I* thought of it first," Jessica added.

The twins grinned at each other.

"And wait till Ginny Lu gets here," Jessica said. "A real country bumpkin! Maybe she'll be here in time for the party. Will we ever impress her!"

"Don't get carried away," Elizabeth warned. "We've had enough of you being *mature* and *sophisticated*."

Jessica grinned. "Wait and see," she said.

Elizabeth groaned. She was sure Jessica and her friends would find plenty of ways to impress Mrs. Waldron's niece from Tennessee.

Will Ginny Lu be accepted by her classmates? Find out in Sweet Valley Twins #22, **OUT OF PLACE.**

THE CLASS TRIP

SWEET VALLEY TWINS SUPER EDITION #1

Join Jessica and Elizabeth in the very first SWEET VALLEY TWINS Super Edition—it's longer, can be read out of sequence, and is full of page-turning excitement!

The day of the big sixth-grade class trip to the Enchanted Forest is finally here! But Jessica and Elizabeth have a fight and spend the beginning of the trip arguing. When Elizabeth decides to make up, Jessica has disappeared. In a frantic search for her sister, Elizabeth finds herself in a series of dangerous and exciting Alice In Wonderland-type of adventures.

☐ 15588-1 $2.95/$3.50 in Canada

Buy them at your local bookstore or use this page to order.

THE
SWEET
VALLEY
TWINS

For two years teenagers across the U.S. have been reading about Jessica and Elizabeth Wakefield and their High School friends in SWEET VALLEY HIGH books. Now in books created especially for you, author Francine Pascal introduces you to Jessica and Elizabeth when they were 12, facing the same problems with their folks and friends that you do.